ANIMAL KINGDOM SERIES

Animal Olympics

Created by Steve Seven

Fully Illustrated Book

Silk Road Publishing

Published by Silk Road Publishing
Text Copyright © 2011 by Silk Road Publishing
Illustration-Copyright © 2011 by Silk Road Publishing
Silk Road Publishing is a division of Silk Road Media Group.

Animal Kingdom Series, Animal Olympics © by Steve Seven
www.AnimalKingdomStory.com

ISBN 978-0-9868519-7-1

Cover design by Eli Achack
Illustrated by S. Salehi
Story Development by M. Najafi

TABLE OF CONTENTS

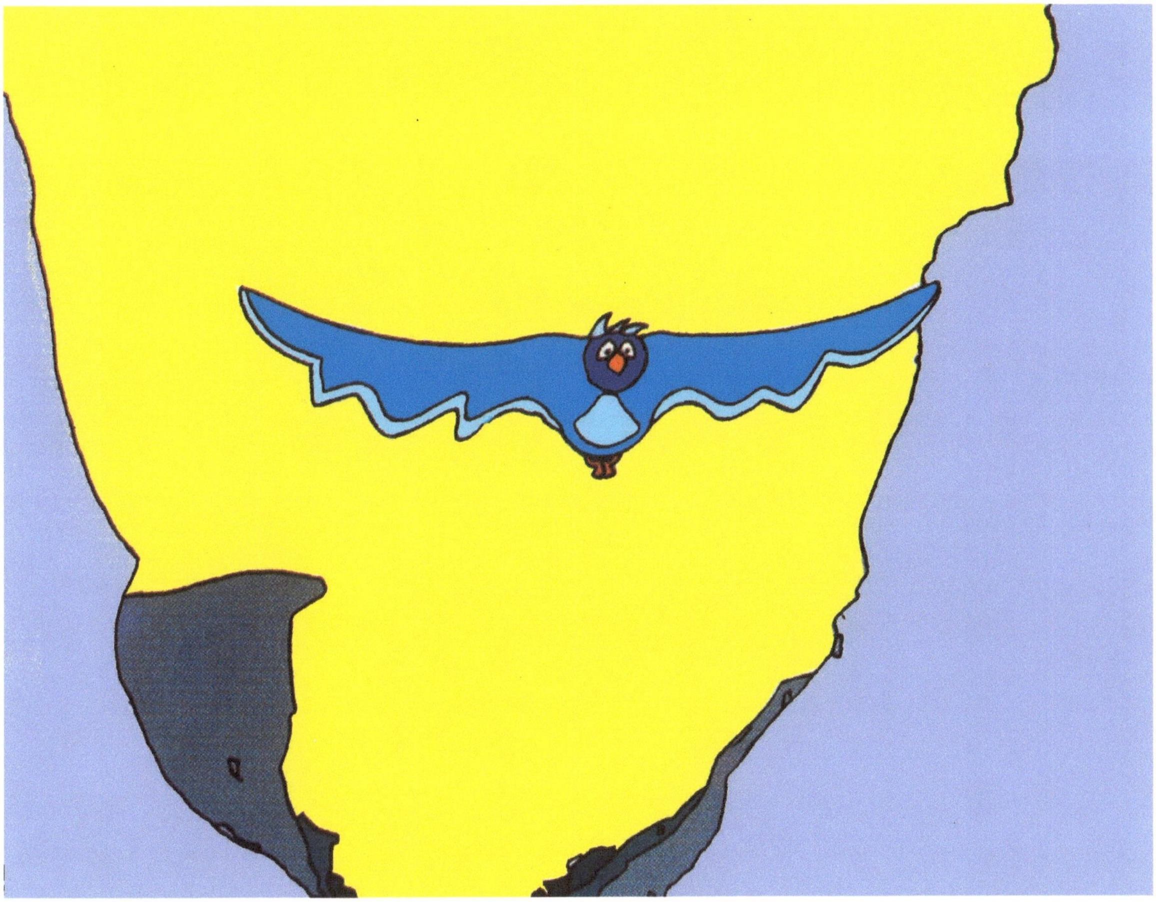

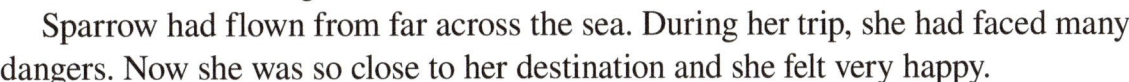

CHAPTER 1: BECAUSE OF FRIENDSHIP

It was a beautiful spring morning. The sun was shining and the sky was blue. Sparrow had been flying for seven days and was feeling very tired. She thought, "I have to reach the Animal Kingdom no matter what."

Sparrow had flown from far across the sea. During her trip, she had faced many dangers. Now she was so close to her destination and she felt very happy.

From high in the sky she could look toward the horizon and see the green fields and forests of Animal Kingdom. Feeling excited, she kept flying toward it.

She was happy. She took a deep breath and thought, "I have reached it at last." She was deep in thought when suddenly she saw a black shadow on the ground. She quickly turned her head and saw a big vulture coming toward her very quickly.

Her tiny heart was beating really fast but she tried to fly even faster. She wanted to reach Animal Kingdom as soon as possible. She began to lose her strength. Suddenly, she heard a voice saying, "In the name of the king; the king of Wolf Kingdom, stop!"

 She did not pay attention and kept on flying. In the distance, she saw a sign that said, "Welcome to the Kingdom of Friendship and Peace, the Animal Kingdom."

She tried to fly faster, but suddenly she felt as if her wings were burning. Then, she lost her senses

The next thing she knew, she was waking and saw a dog looking back at her.

At first, she felt very scared, but the dog said, "Hi my friend. Take it easy. You are in Animal Kingdom now." The dog continued on to say, "I am a border guard in Animal Kingdom. With my binoculars I saw you coming toward our kingdom. Vulture was after you. He shot you with an arrow and you fell to the ground. I quickly crossed the border and brought you to this side."

Sparrow then replied, "You saved my life. Thank you my dear friend." Dog then said, "Now tell me who you are and why you came here."

Sparrow said, "I am a traveler from the other side of the sea. I know a sparrow that has seen your kingdom and told me a lot about it. She said that the Olympics would start in your country soon. I have come from far away to see your kingdom and attend the Olympic Games."

The dog wondered, "You crossed the sky over the Wolf Kingdom?"

Sparrow said, "Yes, I had no choice. I had to fly at night and hide during the day. Just today, I flew in the daylight to reach here sooner and look what happened to me."

Guard Dog went to the window and looked up at the sun. He then told the sparrow, "My friend, the Animal Olympics will start the day after tomorrow and today is the last day of registration. With your wounded wing, you won't be able to reach the city in time to register. It is just too far."

Sparrow became very sad and said, "What a pity!"

Dog then replied, "My dear friend. I am a border guard. I can't leave this place. If I could, I would go and register your name for you myself."

9

Sparrow said nothing. She stood up and walked out of the guard's room. Outside, she saw that there were other dogs guarding the border. She was thirsty so she asked one of them where the nearest stream was.

She couldn't fly with her wounded wing. Guard Dog had wrapped a white cloth around it. She went to the nearby stream to drink. The stream was a nice area with a lot of plants and trees. She felt so very sad.

Suddenly, the bushes on the opposite side of the stream began to move. A deer appeared. As soon as he noticed Sparrow, he said, "Hi my friend. Why are you upset?" Sparrow looked up and said, "Hi, yes I am sad. I have come all the way from the other side of the sea to attend the Olympic Games.
The border guard dog has told me that today is the last day of registration. My wing is injured and I cannot make it in time."

Deer said, "So this is why you are upset. You should not be sad. Sparrow replied, "Oh, if you only knew what I have gone through."

Deer, wanting to help, said, "My friend, do not be upset. Rest here and I will go and register your name for you."

Sparrow thanked him. Deer said goodbye and left quickly. The sun was high in the sky. Deer ran very quickly through the woods and jumped over anything in his way. He had to reach Animal City before sunset.

Deer kept on going until he reached a river. Without stopping, he jumped in and ran through the water. He was just beyond the river when suddenly his wet leg slipped on a stone.

Deer fell hard to the ground. His foot was now in great pain. He stood up and tried to continue on but he found he could not.

Deer's leg was twisted and felt very painful. He thought about Sparrow and said to himself, "No matter what, I must get to Animal City."

He tried to run but could not. He leaned against a tree feeling very sad and hopeless. With all his strength he shouted, "Help. Help. Is there anyone around?"

He listened but no one answered. He stood up again and tried to walk but all he could do was limp. He said to himself, 'Walking like this, I won't even reach Animal City by tomorrow."

Once again, he shouted, "Please help me. Please help me."

Suddenly, he heard a nightingale's voice in the distance. He shouted again in his loudest voice, "Hey my friend, Nightingale Singer."

Nightingale heard the deer's voice. She flew toward him as quickly as she could and sat down beside him on the ground. Nightingale asked, "What happened to you my friend?"

Deer told Nightingale the whole story. Nightingale said, "Don't worry, I will go and register her name for the Olympics and I'll attend the fly game as well."

Deer gave Sparrow's feather to Nightingale and thanked her for her kindness. Nightingale started on her journey and soon disappeared. She passed the jungle and the green field of the animal kingdom.

She had a long way to go. The sun moved closer to the west mountain. In the distance, she could see the Animal City. It made her fly faster.

By the time she reached the city, the sun had almost set. Looking into the distance, she saw the rabbit closing the registration book. She shouted, "Wait. Please wait."

All the animals noticed the nightingale's scream. Nightingale sat on the ground. She was sweating and almost out of breath. Between her breaths she was able to say, "One sparrow….came from….the other side of….the sea and wanted to sign up for…. the Olympic flying….games."

She showed the sparrow's bloody feather and was so tired, she fainted. The sparrow's name though, was the last one on the contestant list.

CHAPTER 2: OLYMPIC SONG

The Animal Olympics were set to begin in two days. Everyone was preparing for the opening ceremonies.

The old lion, still the ruler of Animal Kingdom, was pacing in his room. He was preparing his speech, one that he would give at the opening ceremonies. Wise Owl, who was both a teacher and a member of the Animal Kingdom parliament, had written the speech for him. Lion was standing in front of the mirror and began to speak; "My Friends! The hab…habi….habitants of…"

All of the old lion's teeth had been taken out. That's why Alligator the Dentist had given him a set of artificial (or false) teeth. The problem though, was that these teeth were too loose. Each time he began to speak, the teeth would flop around in his mouth. Determined to finish, he tried again.

"My Friends! The habita…." Again his teeth moved, almost falling out of his mouth. He became frustrated and angry. He took his teeth out and put them aside. In his anger, he exclaimed, "Being a ruler is so hard! The worst part of it is trying to give a speech! That silly owl wrote such a difficult speech for me. How can I give it with these loose teeth? If I had the power, I would have ordered that the alligator's teeth be taken out too!"

He started to give the speech once again, this time with no teeth at all. He started complaining again, "How can I say a speech without any teeth? I am really stuck."

Sergeant Gorilla gathered his troops in a row. They were practicing marching. They were supposed to march in front of the special guests at the beginning of the game.

Giraffe, who was taller than the others, was standing in front. His trousers were too loose for him and he was trying to hold them up with his hand. Gorilla shouted, "What kind of marching is that? You shouldn't be so lazy. Why are you walking like that? Move your hand up. Everybody, everybody…."

As soon as Giraffe moved and took his hand away from his trousers, the trousers fell down. Gorilla saw him and said, "Tell your mum to fix those trousers!"

Giraffe came forward and said, "Yes Sir." He tried to put his hand up to salute Gorilla, but his trousers fell down once again. Gorilla saw this and lost his patience. He said, "Get out of here. Go!"

He held his trousers now with two hands and went to hide behind a tree. He then tried the chubby bear's trousers but they were too tight. He couldn't even pull them up and button them completely.

Gorilla shouted again, "Start Marching." His troops followed his order. In a loud voice, he said, "Haven't you had any food? What kind of marching is that? It's like you are walking in the park. Now move your feet, higher, higher, HIGHER!"

Bear wanted to move his feet higher but as he did, his trousers ripped at the back. Gorilla heard the ripping noise. He turned around and angrily said, "What was that noise?" Bear, who couldn't speak properly, said, "Sir, Sir … my trousers…" gorilla came closer, patted Bear's tummy and said, "Make your tummy smaller." Bear, still thinking about the conversation between Gorilla and Giraffe said, "Yes sir! I will ask my mom to make it smaller for me."

Gorilla became angrier and said, "Are you making fun of me? Now wait and see what I'll do to you." Bear started running away in his worn out trousers and Gorilla chased after him. The other members of the group thought this was so funny, they fell over laughing. One of them said, "Thank God. We can relax now. What is this marching anyway?"

Under the cliff, Fox was preparing for the job he had to do. He was responsible for lighting the Olympic torch. The torch was up high on the cliff. Fox had to throw a fiery arrow and hit the torch to light it. Now, he was practicing with ordinary arrows.

It just so happened that Fox loved to eat cream cakes. He always had some with him and it always seemed that his lips had a little cream on them. Unfortunately, flies loved the cream too and they were always buzzing around Fox. They even tried to eat the cream and cake that were left over on his face.

The flies would make Fox mad and he would tell them to get lost. He got so mad he even tried to hit them with his arrows. In fact, he spent more time doing this than trying to hit the torch.

"Wow! What nice singing.' Nightingale was the master of singing and music in Animal Kingdom. She was standing in front of her group on the platform and was practicing with them. They wanted to sing a special song at the beginning of the Olympic Games. Her group members were Tiny Donkey (who had a lot of talent and a nice voice), Calf (whose father had been a master of music), and Hen (who couldn't really sing at all).

Nightingale said, "All together now….."

The Kingdom of peace
Our Kingdom
The time comes for friendship and peace
Stand from your place

Nightingale interrupted, "No. That's not right. You are making it sound much different than your normal voice. Don't stretch the words too much. It's not an opera."

Tiny Donkey said, "Ok misters, Ok." Again, they started singing;
"The Kingd…."

Nightingale was so bored, "No, no, with this voice, everybody will run away. Now sing slower and smoother."

Calf said, "Misters, do you want me to sing by myself? Then you will see…"
"The Kind….."

Misters Nightingale stopped her singing and said, "For God's sake no! Please just stay quiet."

Finally, the day of the Olympic opening ceremonies arrived. It had been arranged that the old lion would make his speech. A lot of spectators had gathered at the stadium. The stadium was a big square field, surrounded by trees. At one corner, there was a stone platform. The platform was a special place. It also had a smaller stone on it. The old lion stood on the platform behind the small stone and began his speech, "My friends…"

Poor Lion was holding his upper teeth with one hand and his lower teeth with the other to prevent them from falling out during his speech.

"My friends, residents of the Kingdom of Happiness and Peace, we are gathered here to…"

No matter how hard he tried, he couldn't remember the rest. Again, he started, "My friends, residents of the Kingdom of Happiness and Peace, we are gathered here….to…"

Again he couldn't remember it. He became angry and said to Wise Owl who was sitting on the platform, "What kind of speech have you written for me?" Holding his teeth once again he shouted, "Start the games."

The entire crowd started cheering. Old Lion then thought that his speech was very good. He became excited and said, "The thing….the thing…turn on the torch. In the name of peace, in the name of friendship…in the name of…and this kind of thing."

20

The crowd said "Horraaaa…." The old lion became more excited. He forgot that his teeth were loose. He raised his hand upward to command attention. "God bless….oh gosh."

His teeth had come out of his mouth and fell under the platform.

While he was coming down from the platform to find his teeth, he said, "For God's sake, turn on the torch and leave us alone." Owl, who was on top of the platform, said, "His Highness, before turning on the torch, they should sing the Olympic song." Lion, who was still searching for his teeth said,

"Do whatever you want to do, just get it over with."

All over the stadium, the singing could be heard. "The Animal Kingdom .. of .. peace .. it's … Olympic .. time …"

"What an awful song." exclaimed Lion as he put his fingers in his ears. "That's enough," he screamed. He forgot to hold his loose teeth and they fell onto the ground, under his feet. He became so angry he threw them out into the middle of the field. Without any teeth in his mouth he asked, "Is it finished now?"

Owl spoke up and said, "There is still marching and they have to light the torch."

Lion said, "Ah…what is the marching for? Is this a battlefield?" He paused for a second, waved, and said, "Oh well, let the marching begin."

Sergeant Gorilla and his troops started marching.
"One..two…three..four…"

Neither did Giraffe make his trousers smaller, nor did Bear's fat tummy get smaller. Giraffe was holding his trousers with his two hands. Since Bear did not want his trousers to rip, he was trying not to raise his leg too high.

The old lion shouted, "We don't need all this crazy stuff just to turn on the torch. If you don't put stop to all this, I will go and turn on the torch myself."

At last, as the horn sounded, Fox entered the game square. Slowly from his trouser pocket he removed a cream cake and ate it. Next, he took out an arrow and lit its top on fire. Fox stood with pride in front of the cliff and looked at the torch. Everyone was silent and held their breath. Fox expertly adjusted the arrow and aimed it at the torch.

Fox was ready to shoot but in a moment of bad luck, a fly came buzzing along and sat on his nose, hoping to get any leftover cake that might be nearby. Fox tried to bat the fly away with his hand but the fly would not go. Fox became angry and tried to aim the arrow at the fly instead of the torch.

In his anger, he threw the fiery arrow at the fly but it landed on the other side of the green field and hit a tree.

"Fire! Fire! Please help, everyone help! Please help!" Lion noticed that the trees were on fire. He became ready to help. He shouted, "The fire must be extinguished. The jungle is on fire."

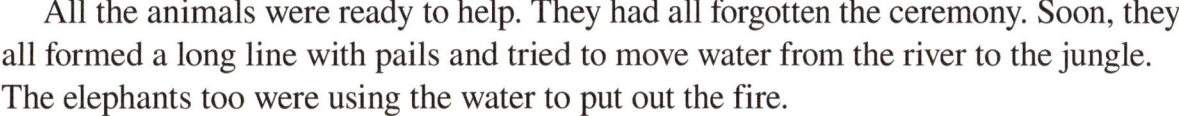

All the animals were ready to help. They had all forgotten the ceremony. Soon, they all formed a long line with pails and tried to move water from the river to the jungle. The elephants too were using the water to put out the fire.

Other animals were throwing soil on the fire. Gravedigger was digging and gathering soil. They were even passing the soil by hand to move it nearer to the fire.

Everyone was busy. Giraffe didn't even think about his falling trousers. The chubby bear wasn't scared anymore either, even if his trousers were falling. Gorilla didn't care about marching anymore. Lion didn't search for his teeth and Fox completely forgot about his sweets. Everyone just wanted to get the fire out. Nothing else was important.

It took until sunset to get the fire out. Everyone was tired. The sky became dark. Everyone went home all black from head to foot.

In the night, everyone turned on a small torch near their home and sang the Olympic song. It could be heard all over, from inside the houses:

The Kingdom of peace
Our Kingdom
It's time for the Olympics and friendship
Stand up now
Hands together
Shoulder to shoulder
Fill the world with peace
The entire world

CHAPTER 3: WHO WAS NUMBER ONE?

The Olympic Games had started. A feeling of happiness spread throughout the Animal Kingdom.

On this particular day, the scheduled sport was weight lifting. The Old Lion was the ruler of Animal Kingdom. Years ago, he had been a weightlifting champion. Even though he had retired, the champion weightlifter of the day would invite him to lift a weight to begin the competition. He was getting old however, and could not lift a real weight.

They had made a light fake weight for him. It looked just like the real one. Even though everyone knew the difference, they did not speak of it.

The weightlifting competitions were held inside a big tent. A lot of animals had gathered there to see the competition. Raven was the reporter for this sport.

He began his report by saying, "And now we would ask that our Kingdom Ruler, Sir Lion, come to the front to begin the competition. He was once a great weightlifter and he is the true master of this sport."

The old lion was still having trouble with his false teeth and was trying to tighten them with some string stretched over his chin and head. His loose teeth would often jump out of his mouth when he tried to talk.

He was wearing his special weightlifting jersey and felt very proud. He walked towards the game field and the audience started clapping. He waved his hand to thank them.

Mr. Donkey was usually in charge of changing the real weights to fake ones for Lion. He would always do this at the beginning of each competition, but on this particular day he was busy and could not be there. He had asked Cow to do this for him but Cow was not all that intelligent.

In all the excitement, Lion moved toward the weightlifting platform as the crowd cheered. First, he checked his teeth to make sure they were not too loose. He stood behind the weights and looked at the crowd. He proclaimed, "Weightlifting is…a….great sport! The first weight I lifted was my father. It was when my mother hit him with her shoe. My father was unconscious so I had to take him to the hospital. I lifted him and carried him on my shoulder."

As he tightened the string on his upper false teeth he said, "The second weight I lifted was my wife. It was a day she wanted to ride a donkey. This was not possible because in our kingdom riding a donkey is banned. I myself had to play the part of the donkey and carry her around…."

Lion was in the middle of this little speech about his early weight-lifting days when suddenly, something from the audience hit his head. He realized it was a shoe, not just any shoe, but his wife's. His wife was tired of his speech and this was her way of telling him to stop.

Lion rubbed the bump on his head and said, "I really love this shoe. This is my mum's shoe that she gave to my wife. Being a weightlifter…..I owe these shoes…."

At this point, his wife shouted from the middle of the audience, "My dear, don't talk too much. It's not good for your heart."

Lion realized that he should stop talking and he whispered to himself, "Oh..oh..again, I ruined every-thing. When I go home, God knows what will hap-pen to me."

Lion ended his speech and stood behind the weights. He made a special pose like a powerful weightlifter. He focused on the weights. Slowly, he bent over and grabbed the middle of the bar with his two hands.

Now Lion was able to lift fake weights easily. He acted as if the weights were real. He made a weightlifting pose thinking that it would fool the audience. He tried to lift the weight but wondered why it was so heavy. He whispered to himself, "What heavy fake weight. Have I become so old that I can't even lift fake weights? What a pity that my youth is gone now….!"

Again, he tried to lift the weights, "…eeeee…..eeeee…..y….."

Again, he couldn't lift the weight. He was starting to sweat. He took a tissue from his pocket and wiped the sweat from his head. He squeezed the tissue and put it back into his pocket. Again, he tried to lift, but he couldn't. He thought that perhaps his teeth were keeping him from focusing. He stood still and tried to keep his cool. He even took his teeth out and put them his pocket.

Again, Lion bent over and grabbed the bar. He tried to force it upward, saying, "What a heavy weight, such a heavy fake weight!" He stood up and thought for a moment. He looked at the audience and said, "Before I lift this weight, I'll tell you a few words about my third weightlifting experience."

Elephant, who had been a weightlifting champion understood what was happening, so he leaned over to Cow and said, "Didn't you change the weights?" Cow replied, "Oh, what a mess! I completely forgot."

By now, Lion was starting to get back pain from lifting so hard. Elephant quickly went to the platform to help and loudly said, "Your Highness, please tell everyone about the third weight you lifted. You see, this weight was me. Back when I was a chubby elephant, I was playing by the river one day. My foot slipped, and I fell into the river. The river was deep, so His Highness quickly, jumped in and lifted me up as if I were a feather. That day he saved my life."

Lion knew this was the truth, and he said, "What good old days."

Elephant continued on, "Now I would like to request that Lion allow us to help with this opening ceremony. We can invite other contestants to come over and help lift the weight to show that we can work together. Will you please let us help you, Your Highness?" Lion, sweating heavily replied, "God bless you, please save me."

Lion then took his teeth from his pocket and tightened them with the string. Bear, Gorilla, and Rhinoceros came forward, and along with Elephant, they all held the bar and help raise it.

Lion held one hand on the bar and the other on his bad back. Everyone cheered as the weight went up. Lion was distracted by all the cheering, and when they put the weight down, he forgot to let go. He fell to the floor and hit his head.
His teeth went flying everywhere. He tried to stand up, but he was clearly frustrated. As he got up, he said, "What is weightlifting? Who invented this sport, anyway?"

The weightlifting competition started. It was very close, but Elephant came in first.

Gold has no value in Animal Kingdom. The most precious thing in Animal Kingdom is a red rose. After every competition, they put a rose ring around the champion's neck.

Raven the Reporter announced, "We now request that His Highness come over and hand out the prizes."

Lion, who was sitting with his wife and son, told his wife, "They just won't leave me alone." His wife replied, "Be careful what you're saying this time. Don't mention my mother, and when you come back, don't forget my shoe."

Lion said, "Your Mother… wow, I forgot she was the fourth and the heaviest I ever lifted." Lady Lion was so angry; she took her other shoe and hit him saying, "You are insulting my mother…."

She hit him so hard that her shoe broke into two pieces. Lion tried to walk down the stairs but now he felt weak. He lost his balance and fell over. Lady Lion screamed, "Oh my God, what have I done? What shall I do? My shoe is broken."

All the animals were gathered around him not knowing what to do. One of them said, "Let's take him to the hospital." His son, Lion Junior was worried. He lifted Lion onto his shoulder. The other animals cleared the way as he carried his father off.

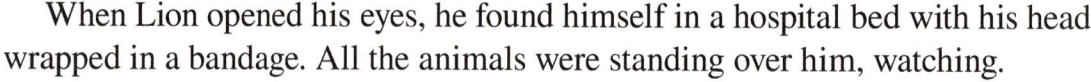

When Lion opened his eyes, he found himself in a hospital bed with his head wrapped in a bandage. All the animals were standing over him, watching.

Lion smiled and said, "Give me my teeth." He put his teeth back in and looked around, but he couldn't see his wife. "Where is my wife?" he asked.

His son replied, "Mother is searching for her shoe, the one she threw at your head during the speech." Cow was standing in the corner and commented, "That shoe made Lion Junior into a weightlifter as well. It was he who lifted you and brought you here."

Lion said, "God bless my father, he was a weightlifter as well."

Again, everyone laughed. Lion asked, "Who was won the competition? It was Elephant wasn't it?" Elephant was there. He came closer and put the rose ring he had won around Lion's neck, saying, "You are number one, the one who carries the weight of responsibility on your shoulders….the responsibility of peace, friendship and freedom, you are number one."

By now, Lion's eyes were full of tears. By the time Doctor Goat came in to ask everyone to leave and let Lion rest, all the animals were crying.

CHAPTER 4: LIFE-LONG CHAMPION

The Olympic Games continued on with great excitement. There was so much happiness all over Animal Kingdom.

In one small corner of the Kingdom, two animals sat together making a plan. One of them was Foxy and the other Foxo. They were brothers. Foxy was a gymnastics champion and Foxo a ski champion. They were not anyone's enemy, but they were a little tricky.

Foxy said, "We have to win this year. Mima cannot be the winner."

Foxo said, "Mima is a clever monkey. He is a master gymnast." To this, Foxy replied, "I have to be champion no matter what."

Foxo said, "We have no choice, we have to cheat."

Foxy asked, "What kind of cheating brother?"

Foxo thought for a second and said, "I will go and ask Spider."

Foxy: "Spider?"

Foxo: "Yes, I will catch some flies and then go and visit Spider."

Spider was sitting in the bushes, waiting in one corner of his web. He was bored and started to complain, saying to himself, "What kind of life is this? I sit here all day just looking at this web and waiting to catch a fly. I am tired of this life."

Then he started singing:

Fly oh fly oh fly
You're killing me, it's enough
I am dying of hunger here
Fly please help me

Then Spider heard a voice, "What a nice voice you have, Mr. Spider."
"Wow Foxo the champion, what brings you this way? You have remembered me."
Foxo replied, "Why do you talk like this Spider? I am always thinking of you."

"What's up," said Spider, "Not thinking of cheating again, are you?"

"No plan. I brought some flies for you."

Foxo threw three flies into Spider's web. Spider was very hungry and started eating. While he enjoyed his meal, he asked, "So, what's new?"

Foxo replied, "I need you to do a favor for me." Spider was curious, "What favor?"

Foxo said, "Tomorrow, my brother, Foxy must compete in gymnastics. You know Mima. He won't let anyone else win. This year, I want my brother to be champion… and you will have another fly for your breakfast as well."

Spider thought about it and asked, "What shall I do?"

Foxo gave him his plan. Since Spider really liked the taste of flies, he accepted.

The gymnastics competition was beginning. The large field was all set. Lion, the kingdom ruler, was there to watch. His wife was with him as well. They were sitting in an area for special guests.

The competition had three parts, floor routine, uneven bars, and parallel bars. Mima, Foxy, and Tiger were all competing. Tiger did not score well. Foxy was in the lead, but now it was Mima's turn.

Everyone was sure he would win. Mima stood in front of the audience and bowed. He was just about to begin but suddenly, he felt a tickling. He started to laugh out loud.

Lion thought that Mima was laughing at him so he checked his own appearance. He even checked his false teeth. He then whispered to his wife, "Everything seems ok, so why is the monkey laughing?"

Lady Lion looked at him and said, "Go look at yourself in the mirror and you will laugh."

Mima started laughing very loud again. Lion looked at his wife carefully and nervously said, "Maybe he is laughing at you."

With this, Lady Lion became angry and said, "How dare he do that, I will straighten him out myself."

She took off her shoe. Lion took her hand and said, "That's enough, I cannot buy shoes everyday to let you hit everyone's head. I do not have enough money for that."

Since Lady Lion had no other choices, she grabbed the string that Lion used to keep his teeth in place. Next, she took out Lion's teeth and threw them towards the field where Mima was. The teeth hit Mima on the head.

Mima still didn't know why he was laughing. He tried to do his floor routine but all he could do was a series of crazy movements.

Lady Lion whispered, "What is he doing? Is this some new sport we don't know about?" Lady Lion was so angry. She cried out, "Look, he made fun of me. What kind of husband are you? You should have him punished?" Lion, now without his teeth, could not speak well, but said, "What are you saying my dear? Laughing is not a crime. I do not use my power in this way anymore."

Lady Lion complained again, "I wish I had married the wolf. I rejected many marriage proposals because of you."

Lion slowly whispered, "The way you keep hitting me with your shoe, I wish you had married the wolf too. heeee … heeee …. heee"

Mima still could not do well in the floor routine. Parallel bars came. He kept laughing and still did crazy movements that no one could understand. At the end, he tried to do a spin, but felt more tickling and fell and landed on his head.

The audience watched him and started screaming. While Mima was still lying on the floor, Lion stood up to see to him, but he tripped and slipped down the stairs. His upper teeth also fell out. Spider, who had been tickling Mima, came out and hid in the corner. Lion managed to get to Mima and angrily said, "Take him to the hospital."

The result was clear. Foxy was the winner.

Foxo caught some flies and took them to Spider. When he got there, Spider was sitting in the corner feeling sad. Foxo thanked him saying, "Well done. You have done a great job."

The spider did not answer. Foxo said, "I have a few flies for you."

Spider looked up. Angrily he said, "I don't want the flies. If I had known something would happen to Mima, I would never have done such a thing."

Foxo replied, "Nothing happened. Now have your flies. They will make you feel better."

Spider became even angrier. He cried out, "I almost killed somebody just for a few flies.
This is ridiculous. I won't eat anything until I know Mima is well."

Foxo said nothing and walked away. He started to think about the skiing competition that he himself might win.

Mima was wearing a bandage on his head and was resting in the hospital. He had received a hard hit to the head and he could not even stand up. Spider felt bad for Mima. He crept quietly into Mima's room and spun his web to keep the flies away from him.

Doctor and Nurse Goat took care of Mima. After one night, he felt better but his head still hurt. He began asking about the results of the Olympic Games. He asked the nurse about the latest news.

She replied, "Today there is bad news." Mima was shocked. Sadly, Nurse Goat explained, "At Pearl Mountain, several skiers are trapped in a ski lift cabin on the other side of the mountain. There is so much snow, nobody can rescue them."

When the nurse left the room, Mima started thinking. The thought of the possible death of the animals made him shiver. He tried to stand but his head was spinning. He slowly crept out of the hospital. The doctor wanted him to rest for another 24 hours but he could not. He had to reach Pearl Mountain as soon as possible. He went home, collected his ropes and started out.

The mountain was covered in snow. That was why they called it Pearl Mountain. A lot of animals were gathered at the bottom of the mountain but none could do anything. Lion was restless. He was pacing back and forth and when he saw Mima, said, "You should be in hospital, what are you doing here?"

Mima pleaded, "Your Highness, please let me help? I am OK. Please let me help save my friend's life. I have a plan. I can reach the lift and tie the cabin with ropes. Others who are here can pull the rope and bring the cabin to the top of the mountain to safety."

Lion replied, "It's really dangerous, I'm scared. If you are still dizzy, you might fall and it's 300 feet to the ground.

Mima still wanted to try. He said, "You know there is no choice and I am a skilled tight-rope walker."

Mima did as he said he would and soon, Mima and the other animals were on top of the mountain with the lift. Mima walked along the cable down to the cabin. All the animals were very nervous, afraid that Mima would fall to his death. Mima himself was starting to feel dizzy again, so he moved slowly.

Finally, he reached the cabin and tied the rope to it. He then went back to the top, again slowly so he would not fall. When he finally reached the top, he fell to the ground exhausted. All the animals

quickly grabbed the rope and pulled the cabin upward. The cabin slowly moved along to the top and luckily, everyone survived.

In the end, the ski games were held with Foxo coming out the winner. He had been stuck on the lift and felt very lucky to be alive.

When the prizes were awarded, Mima attended with a bandaged head. The reporters announced Foxo as the winner. Foxo went to the platform. They put the rose ring on him and he felt very happy, but he thought for a second and then hesitated. He looked at the audience. He walked into the crowd and went to Mima. He took the valuable rose ring and placed it around Mima's neck. He then carried Mima on his shoulder and shouted, "Life-long champion, life-long champion."

The audience agreed and joined in the shouting and cheering for Mima as well.

CHAPTER 5: GOOD-BYE OLYMPICS

It was the last few days of the Olympic Games and the archery competition was about to begin. The main contestants were Fox the Archer and Cute Cat.

Fox really loved to eat cream cakes. In fact, there were always so many bits and pieces stuck on his face that flies would be attracted to him. They were always buzz-ing around him and this time he had planned to keep them away by wearing helmet and cage that he had made.

Cute Cat always carried a bot-tle of drink with him and before any competition he always took a few sips. He also loved to chase mice, and that is why the mice didn't want him to win the game.

Misha led the group that was against Cute Cat. He made a plan to make him lose. He would put some drops of sleeping medicine in Cat's drinking bottle just before the competition. This would make him sleepy and dizzy and miss the target.

Misha hid himself in a closet in the athletes changing room. When Cute Cat came in to change and laid his bottle down, Misha came out from the closet and started to add the drops of medicine to the bottle. He was in such a hurry to add the drops though without being caught, he accidentally added all the medicine.

During the archery competition, Fox felt very confident with his special helmet on. He focused and threw his first arrow. It hit the target just a little from the center.

Next, it was Cute Cat's turn. He took a few sips from his bottle. As soon as he did, everything seemed to look different. He even thought the target was changing its place. He tried to move with it and then shot his arrow. The arrow did not go near the target. Instead, it hit the wooden wall behind King Lion's head.

Lion and his wife, Lady Lion, had come to watch the competition. Colonel Tiger, the leader of Animal Kingdom's army, saw what was happening and quickly went out onto the field. Fearing that Cute Cat had tried to hit King Lion, he arrested him immediately. Meanwhile, the audience had gathered around the wall where the arrow had hit and were busy talking.

"He intended to assassinate Lion."

"No. No way, he cannot even wipe his own nose."

"He must be an enemy spy."

"Maybe he lost his balance…………………"

Colonel Tiger brought Cat to King Lion and said, "Sir, he is a traitor. He intended to assassinate you. If you allow me, I will sort him out right away."

King Lion, while still trying to tighten his loose teeth with the string over his head, said, "Oh Colonel, why hurt him? Let's see why the poor fellow did such a thing."

As soon as Cat saw the lion running toward him, he kissed him on his bald head. Not being able to see well he said, "Oh my dear aunt, how I missed you so much."

The old lion was surprised. Angrily he said, "Dear aunt? Do I look like your aunt?" Lady Lion standing beside him said, "Darling, I myself sometimes mistake you for my grandmother." Lion replied, "You have the right my lady."

Cat noticed Lady Lion. Looking at King Lion, he said, "Aunty! What is this monkey saying? Is he your new husband?" King Lion thought this really funny and started to laugh, saying, "What a lovely cat! He recognized my husband so quickly. Heh..he… he..monkey….Husband…"

Suddenly, a hit from a shoe regained his attention. Lady Lion was screaming, "Are you making fun of me? Now, I will sort both of you…bang..bang…."

At last, Colonel Tiger calmed everyone down. The cat however, was still unable to see straight and held onto the Colonel saying, "My dear aunty, will you buy a lollipop for me?"

51

Colonel Tiger spoke to Lion saying, "He is crazy. He should never be allowed to have a bow and arrow in his hands. I am dressed in this uniform with all these medals and he even calls me aunty. Believe me, if it wasn't for you, I would have hit him so hard, he wouldn't even be able to taste sweets again."

Wise Owl, a teacher and a member of parliament, came closer and said, "I guess he is not feeling well. We should take him to the hospital.

At the hospital, Goat the doctor took some blood samples and sent them to the lab for testing. When the results came back, Goat said, "This cat was drugged with a very dangerous poison. Unfortunately, we do not have any remedy for it. This cat will die very soon."

The old lion asked with sadness, "Why was he poisoned? Was it by accident?" Doctor Goat replied, "I don't know. Maybe he intended to use a special medicine to boost his strength. But he used the wrong medicine.

Everyone was talking about Cat's sickness. The only known cure was the extract from a plant called "life", which wasn't available in Animal Kingdom.

At the Olympic Games, there was a sparrow that had come a long way from the other side of the sea. She had made it through the wolf's sky. With help from others, she managed to reach Animal Kingdom. She had traveled through many countries on her way.

When she heard of Cat's sickness, she quickly went to the hospital. Many animals were gathered in the yard talking. Lion sat with a very sad look, talking to the others as well.

Sparrow went to the lion and said, "I know where we could find the life plant."

Everybody turned their head quickly toward Sparrow. Sparrow continued, "On the other side of the sea, there is a small town. Once upon a time, I had a nest on the roof of a shopping mall. Over there, I saw an old man who had this plant in his shop. Human beings use this plant's extract to get rid of the wrinkles on their faces."

As soon as the old lion heard this, he said, "Shhhhh say it lower ... if my lady hears that, she will ask all the animals to go and get that for her."

Wise Owl said, "Now what shall we do? That is too far from here." Lion thought a little and said, "Quickly, ask Eagle to come over here."

After a few minutes, Eagle, leader of the Air Force appeared in the sky over the hospital. Slowly, he landed in the yard.

King Lion told him the story about the cat and the life plant. The eagle said, "I will go there myself." Sparrow said, "I will go with you to show you the way. But our problem is how to get the extract. It is in the old man's shop. When he closes the shop, he even closes the metal shutter as well. "

Everyone became quiet and started thinking. Misha was there as well. Nobody knew it was his entire fault. He felt very guilty. His conscience bothered him so much; he stepped forward and said, "I guess I can help. I will get into the old man's shop by going through the roof. I will then open a way for others to enter."

Sparrow felt happy with this and said, "Yes. That is it. We have to take Misha as well."

In an hour, Sparrow, Eagle, and Misha were ready for their trip. They took a small basket to take some necessary things. They even let Misha sit inside to be carried. Eagle gripped the basket with his powerful claws and started flying. Sparrow flew alongside as well.

They had to pass through the sky over the wolf's kingdom. A few years back, King Wolf, along with a group of wolves, jackals, and hyenas had taken over this part of animal kingdom and ruled it themselves. Everyone was terrified to go near there. They even had help from the vultures who controlled the sky.

Eagle flew along without stopping or even feeling tired. Misha was still inside the basket and felt very stressed. He thought to himself, "What if Eagle has to fight the vultures? He might lose his grip on the basket and I will fall to my death in pieces…. There is no way. Cat's life is in danger and it's my entire fault."

In the distance, Eagle saw a dark moving cloud. Sparrow screamed, "The vultures... the vultures….!"

The black cloud was certainly a group of vultures and they fully intended to attack.

Eagle shouted, "Hey Sparrow, come over here and sit on top of the basket. I want to fly high."

Sparrow sat on the basket and held tight. Eagle started flying higher and higher; so high the vultures could not see them anymore. After a few hours, they felt safe enough to fly lower again.

Sparrow then flew further ahead on her own. They went on until they reached the city. They landed beside a river that flowed near a mountain. Feeling tired, they rested awhile and then started to fly again.

It was almost dark by the time they reached the city. People were on their way home from the shopping mall. Even the old man was beginning to close his shop. Eagle and his two friends sat on the roof waiting. The old man finally closed up and then Misha started.

After a while, Misha made a small hole in the roof. He looked down through the hole. A small light from the corner made it bright enough to see around the shop. He then noticed a pan

full of liquid. Sparrow looked through the hole as well. She became excited. "This is the extraction pan and that's the life plant extract in it," she said.

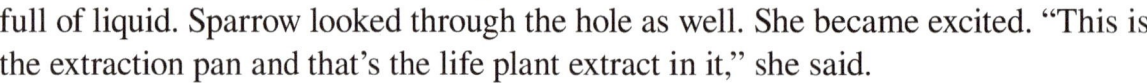

Misha took a small bottle and tied a string around its neck. He lowered the bottle through the hole and let it sink into the pan. The bottle filled with the extract and Misha quietly brought it back up. They finally had the extract.

They felt very happy and grateful. They even threw a rose they had brought with them down through the hole.

Back in Animal Kingdom, the Olympic Games were coming to an end. The competition set for the final day was all about flying. Birds would compete in two types of flying; "stamina flying" and "high flying." Sparrow was registered for the first and Eagle for the second, but neither of them was there.

Cat's sickness was making everyone sad. Most of the animals were visiting him at the hospital instead of going to watch the Games. The old Lion was worried as well. By now the cat was just lying on the bed, unconscious.

Goat the doctor said, "If we do not give him the extract today, he will die….."

Everyone was staring at the sky. Hours passed but there was still no news. They were losing hope when suddenly Raven, who was sitting on the hospital's roof, shouted, "They're coming…they're coming…"

Everyone screamed with happiness and excitement. All three were very tired. Goat got the extract and fed it to Cat as quickly as he could. Everyone waited with excitement to see if it would work.

Suddenly, the voice of Lady Lion could be heard down the hall; "Where is the old man…? " The old lion said, "Oh..oh…oh my…my angel has arrived." Lady Lion entered the room carrying a pan of her own. "Why didn't you tell me this extract would remove wrinkles from my face? Now give me some of it."

Lion said, "My dear lady, we have given it to the cat to …"

Before he finished, she interrupted, hit him on the head with her spoon saying, "Ahh you are never thinking of me…"

Lion touched his head and said, "Oh you are still very beautiful my dear. I even dream of you every night. Can't you hear me screaming in my sleep?"

Lady Lion threw down her pan and spoon and left the room in anger. Everyone's attention returned to the cat again.

Suddenly, a nurse shouted, "He is conscious. He is conscious."

Cat opened his eyes. He saw all his friends and relatives around him. Sleepily he said, "My dear aunt, you are here as well?"

Old Lion heard this and said, "Oh no, he is still confused."

An old cat came near the bed and said, "Yes, your aunty...I am here." Lion breathed a sigh of relief and said, "I was really worried. I thought he was confusing me with his aunt again."

Meanwhile, Pigeon came to Lion and said, "Your Highness, all the matches are finished. Everyone in the stadium is waiting for you. Don't you want to come?"

Lion asked. "Is my wife there?"

Pigeon: "Yes Sir Lion."

Lion: "Oh...Oh...give me that pan please...."

All the animals were gathered at the stadium. The Olympic Games were finally finished. Each member of the audience had a red rose in their hand.

Old Lion took the pan his wife had thrown at him and put it on his head to protect himself from further hits from her shoe.

Sparrow and Eagle entered the stadium as well. As they did, roses thrown by the audience rained down on them. The birds who had won the flying competitions flew overhead as well and presented them with the championship rose ring they had won.

Lion, who was looking on from his special seat, asked Wise Owl, "Where is Misha?"

Misha didn't attend the ceremony. He was still feeling guilty for what he had done. The owl was just about to answer Lion when Cute Cat entered the stadium with Misha on his shoulder. Everyone started cheering again.

Suddenly, Cute Cat took an arrow with a flag on it and placed it on his bow. He shot it into the sky. It came down and stuck into a tree in the corner of the stadium. The flag unrolled and everyone could see it. The entire animal kingdom stood up and started singing the Farewell Olympic Song:

Our home because of you
Becomes full of smiles and happiness
Olympic Games you gave us
The message of peace
Goodbye Olympics
Come to us again
Bring peace and happiness
To our home.

59

Other Animal Olympics Formats and Versions:

Ebook:
PDF Format ISBN: 978-1-927060-00-1
Epub Format ISBN: 978-0-9868519-9-5
Kindle Format ISBN: 978-0-9868519-8-8

Audio Book Formats:
Audio CD with backstage interview and music video DVD Package ISBN: 978-0-9868519-0-2
Male and Characters Voices, MP3 Download ISBN: 978-0-9868519-4-0
Female and Characters Voices, MP3 Download ISBN: 978-0-9868519-3-3
Female Narrator only, MP3 Download ISBN: 978-0-9868519-2-6
Male Narrator onlyMP3 Download, ISBN: 978-0-9868519-1-9

Multimedia (Interactive)
DVD-ROM (Windows) Including book, music video,
backstage scenes and audio books ISBN: 978-0-9868519-6-4
DVD-ROM (Mac) Including book, music video,
backstage scenes and audio books ISBN: 978-1-927060-01-8

Music Track:
Animal Olympic Official Music track, Follow Me, ISBN: 978-0-9868519-5-7

Music Video:
Animal Olympic Official Music Video, Follow Me, ISBN: 978-1-927060-02-5